Lidija Šimkutė
Translated into Japanese by Kōichi Yakushigawa
SOMETHING IS SAID / POEMS

リジア・シムクーテ 作
薬師川虹一 訳
詩集　何かが語られる

何かが語られる

2016 年 4 月 15 日　第 1 刷発行
著　者　リジア・シムクーテ
翻訳者　薬師川虹一
発行人　左子真由美
発行所　㈱竹林館
〒 530-0044　大阪市北区東天満 2-9-4　千代田ビル東館 7 階 FG
Tel 06-4801-6111　Fax 06-4801-6112
郵便振替 00980-9-44593　　URL http://www.chikurinkan.co.jp
印刷・製本　㈱国際印刷出版研究所
〒 551-0002　　大阪市大正区三軒家東 3-11-34
© Lidija Šimkutė
　　Kōichi Yakushigawa　　2016 Printed in Japan
ISBN978-4-86000-329-6　C0098
定価はカバーに表示しています。落丁・乱丁はお取り替えいたします。

SOMETHING IS SAID

Lidija Šimkutė

Translation: Kōichi Yakushigawa
First published by CHIKURINKAN Apr. 2016
2-9-4-7FG, Higashitenma, Kita-ku, Osaka, Japan
http://www.chikurinkan.co.jp
Printed by KOKUSAIINSATSU Osaka, Japan
All rights reserved

SOMETHING IS SAID

何かが語られる

OUTLIVING PEOPLE AND TREES

Tomas Venclova

Lidija Šimkutė holds a special place in Lithuanian literature. She was born in Lithuania but lives and matured in Australia where she was educated. I doubt if there is another Lithuanian poet who belongs to two regions which are separated by the earth's diameter. Lidija has been a persistent traveller, is well informed about other continents and has visited forty countries. It seems she lives in a space between nations and continents. One normally thinks of a sedentary Lithuanian who is attached to his/ her birthplace and plot of land. There are countless myths relating to kinship with the land that have inspired writers but have often tumbled – and continue to tumble into tiresome reading. Lidija belongs to a new generation that doesn't fear globalization and feels at ease in any country. In the near future, without doubt all Lithuanians will feel like this. It is no wonder that her poetry is translated into fifteen languages and she has represented Lithuanian and Australian poetry at various international poetry festivals. Her poems have been and are admired by many – from Marija

人を超え樹を超えて生きる

トマス・ヴェンクロヴァ

リジア・シムクーテはリトアニアの文学史の中でも特別な位置を占めている。彼女はリトアニアで生まれたがオーストラリアで暮らし教育を受け、そこで成熟した。まるで地球の反対側に在る二つの地域を股にかけたリトアニアの詩人が彼女以外にいるだろうか。リジアは永遠の旅人であり、ヨーロッパ以外の大陸を知りつくし、四十を超える国々を訪れているのだ。まるで彼女は国や大陸を超越した世界に住んでいるようなのだ。リトアニア人と言えば普通その人の生まれ育った土地にしっかり根付いている人を想像するだろう。その土地とのきずなにまつわる無数の神話があり、それが作家にインスピレーションを与えてきたのだが、同時にそれが変わり映えのしない退屈な作家を生みだしているのかもしれない。リジアは新しい世代の人種なのだ。彼らはグローバリゼーションを恐れない。そしてどこの国に居ても安心立命していられる。近い将来全てのリトアニアの人々がこういう心情になるだろうことは疑いのないところである。だから彼女の詩が十五カ国語に翻訳され、様々な国での国際詩祭で、リトアニアとオーストラリアを代表する詩人として受け入れられているのは驚くにあたらない。彼女の詩は、

Gimbutas to the Nobel laureate J. M. Coetzee, from Lithuanian poets Marcelijus Martinaitis and Antanas A. Jonynas to the well known Australian writer David Malouf, Austrian and Japanese poets Christian Loidl and Koichi Yakushigawa.

Allegiance to one's motherland is first and foremost allegiance to its language. But even here, things are not so simple. Lidija Šimkutė is both a Lithuanian and Australian poet. She writes in Lithuanian and English. If a poem comes to her mind in English, it immediately finds a Lithuanian version, if it comes in Lithuanian – the English version follows. They are not always direct translations: every language dictates somewhat different metaphors. It can be said that Lidija lives not only in a space between continents, but also in a space between languages: the fullness of her texts is displayed at intersections of both versions. The point which belongs to both versions – and to neither – where not only the languages intersect but also literary traditions: Lithuanian archetypes fall into a hermetic Western lyrical context.

Someone has said that present day poetry is closer to Li Bo than to Dryden – a form of writing that is laconic, minimalist and meditative, rather than voluble, didactic and rational. I feel that both forms are

マリヤ・ギンブタス（リトアニアの考古学者・1921～1994）
からノーベル賞詩人 J. M. コウジィ、リトアニアの詩
人マーセリアス・マルチネイティスやアンタナス・
A. ジョイナスから有名なオーストラリアの作家デイ
ヴィッド・マーロフ、オーストリアの詩人クリスチャ
ン・ロイデル、日本の詩人コウイチ・ヤクシガワにい
たるまで、多くの詩人たちから賞賛されてきている。
　母国への忠誠は第一であり、母国語への忠誠はさら
に強い。しかしこの点において、ことはそれほど単純
ではない。リジア・シムクーテはリトアニアの詩人で
あり同時にオーストラリアの詩人でもある。リトアニ
ア語で書き、英語でも書く。英語で生まれた詩は同時
にリトアニア語の詩になり、リトアニア語で生まれれ
ばそれは同時に英語の詩にもなる。それらは必ずしも
直訳ではない。あらゆる国語が同じメタファーを使う
ことはあり得ないだろう。リジアは幾つもの大陸にま
たがって生きているだけでなく、幾つもの国語にまた
がって生きているのである。したがって、彼女の完全
な詩は二つの言葉の重なる処に在ると言えるだろう。
英語、リトアニア語のどちらにも属し、どちらだけに
も属さない場所、言語のみならず、文学の伝統も交差
しあうところ、そこではリトアニアの原型とヨーロッ
パの複雑な祖形とが融合している。
　現代詩はドライデンより李白に近づいていると言っ
た人がいる。つまり、言葉を尽くし、合理的に説明す

essential – if only one of these remained, the tension which allows expansion and variety would disappear. However, it's evident that Lidija Šimkutė leans towards minimalism which she associates with impromptu, improvisation, the sphere of freedom. In this collection of poems *Something Is Said* half a hundred poems consist of more or less three hundred lines, barely a couple of thousand words (an exception is a lengthy stream of consciousness monologue *Perhaps It's a Dream* presumably about the death of someone she is close to). Lidija Šimkutė is inclined to an Oriental poetry tradition where words are nearly „washed away", merge with a gesture, a dance movement, a momentary ritual. The poems transform into a Kyoto garden surrounded by stones and sand circles that allude to silence and refer to something quintessential which cannot be completely comprehended and fully expressed in words.

This is a radical and even an extreme path to take. As in all radical forms there lies an underlying risk. Minimalist poems can be concentrated and dynamic, balancing on borders of disappearance, rise in a memorable image, a psychological picturesque gesture, an aphorism – like Basho and the mentioned Li Bo. They can also be banal, saying little. The multilayered

るというより、できる限り言葉を切り詰め、想いを解放する詩なのである。勿論このどちらも重要な要素である。もし片方だけになれば、広がりと多様性とを生み出す集中力が失われてしまうだろう。とはいえ、リジア・シムクーテが短詩形に依っていることは明らかであり、それを即興性という解放区に繋げているのである。『何かが語られる』というこの詩集においておよそ五十篇の詩が三百行前後から成り立っていて、およそ二・三千語前後しか使われていない（彼女とつながりの深い人の死を悼む、意識の流れ風の独語詩、「夢であっくほしい」が唯一の例外だろう）。リジア・シムクーテは伝統的な東洋の詩にも傾倒している。そこでは言葉は「洗い流され」、身振りやダンスの、一瞬の儀式に似た動きと融合する。彼女の詩は石と白砂とに囲まれた京都の庭園に変貌する。それは静寂の表象であり、五感を超えた世界、言葉では決して完全に説明し表現しきれない、世界なのである。

　これは過激であり、極端な路線である。あらゆる過激な形には危険が潜んでいるものだ。短詩形の詩は濃縮された躍動感があり、破綻の境界でバランスを取り、鮮明なイメージとなって立ち上がり、心理的華麗なイメージ、警句的となる。芭蕉風であり、李白風なのである。だがそれはまた浅薄なものにもなり得るだろう。重層的な言い回しは不毛の劇場に堕落するかもしれない——東洋の古典的作家を模倣しようとした西洋の詩

texts can fall into a sterile arena – as is the case with many Western poets who imitate Eastern classical writers. It seems that poetry can come from nothing and it is possible to write about nothing. Spring water that doesn't have colour or taste but quenches thirst can become distilled water – without colour or taste, more precisely – tasteless. Lidija Šimkutė is not afraid to take a risk and hence often reaches her goal – producing a lucid, elegant and authentic text.

In these texts – modern versions of tankas or haiku – „paper soaks up the remains of an instance", the boundary disappears between the object and the subject. They both (but only just) disappear. Body – skin, „the moons of fingernails", bone and breath flow into silence. In silence sound is dormant. In grammar, the first person seeks the second – and finds him, even though it seems an impossibility. The landscape implies transformation or a point of climax.

The landscapes of Lidija Šimkutė's poems are very variable – including eucalyptus from Australia, Vienna's Prater, streets of Budapest and a bar in New York City which is very accurately portrayed. The most realistic portrayals are of Vilnius and the Baltic (in these Lithuanian collages one can hear a particularly personal angst and tones of danger). The poems merge

人たちのように。詩は『無』から生まれるようにも思われるし、事実『無』について書くことは可能である。泉の水は色も味もないが、渇きを癒すことはできる。と同時にそれは色も味もない蒸留水になることもできる。つまり、はっきり言えば不味い水なのだ。リジア・シムクーテは危険を恐れない、だからこそ目標を達成し、上品で煌めく純正の詩を生み出せるのだ。

このような表現──短歌や俳句の現代版──「言葉の言い残したものをページの空白が吸収する」(本文43頁参照) ような作品の中では主体と客体との間の境界は消滅する。両者とも正に消滅するのだ。肉体──肌、爪の月型、骨も呼吸も静寂の中に流入する。静寂の中で音は静止する。文法では一人称は二人称を求め、たとえ不可能にみえてもそれを見つける。与えられた風景は変形あるいは臨界点を意味しているのだ。

リジア・シムクーテの詩における風景──オーストラリアのユーカリの木、ブダペストの街並み、ニューヨークのバーなど、きわめて正確に描かれている。もっともリアリスティックなのはヴィルニウスの市街とバルチック海の風景だろう。これらのリトアニア的コラージュの中にきわめて個人的な不安と恐怖感を聞きとることができる。彼女の詩は音楽と共に映像を伴って迫ってくる。「私はしばしば古代の民謡の世界に回帰する」と彼女は言う。こういう古代の韻律の形を取ることによって、彼女は、音が作曲家の意図から離れ

with paintings as well as music. The author has said: „often I return to very archaic folk music". In this form of ancient music there is an attempt to reach a point whereby sound composes itself without the intension of the composer. And when this music is achieved, quoting Lidija Šimkutė, it „outlives people and trees".

WHERE CITIES END

— nests fly

ominous bird song
emerges as grass sings

music outlives
people
and trees

て自らを形成してゆくような場にまで到達しようとしているのである。このような旋律の世界に到達すると、彼女の詩を引用するなら、詩は「人や樹を超えて生きる」のである。

街が終わる処では

── *鳥の巣は翔び*

不吉な鳥の歌が現れ
草たちが歌う

調べは人や
樹を
超えて生きる

Tomas Venclova : トマス・ヴェンクロヴァ（1937─）
リトアニアの詩人・翻訳家・文学者。人種差別・暴力等に積極的に反対し、2012 年には杉原財団より寛容賞〈Man of Tolerance of the Award〉を受ける。

CORNFLOWER SKY

In the middle of sky's temple
blooms a flower

KABIR

矢車草の空

蒼穹の伽藍の真っ只中に
　　　一輪の花が咲く

KABIR

KABIR：カビール
15 世紀のインドの詩人・宗教家。ヒンドゥー教にもイスラム教にも
批判的であった。

A BIRD CALL

pierces
first flicker of light

sun hides
its gold
in the trees

鳥の叫びが

切り裂く
来光の最初の煌き

太陽はその
黄金の光を
木立の中に隠す

HOW BEAUTIFUL

are the beginnings
of things

I watch
the pale of the moon
in the dawn of the sky

do not ask why

なんと美しいのだろう

すべて
物事の始まりは

曙の空に架かる
青ざめた月を
私は見つめる

何故かは知らねど

TIME LINGERS

to wash away words

while the leaf dreams
inside the leaf

the flower lifts its head
from its scattered sleep
and meets the sun

時はそぞろに

言葉を洗い流す

その間にも木の葉は
木の葉の胎内で夢見ている

散乱する眠りの中から
花はその頭をもたげ
太陽を見上げる

SCARVED WOMEN

cuddle newborn loaves
to their breasts

weave wide skirts
through potato
and onion sacks

lettuce head girls
        arrange
fresh picked flowers

embroider dreams
with sun thread laughter

スカーフを巻いた女たちが

出来たてのパンを
胸に抱き

じゃがいもと
玉ねぎの袋で
広いスカートを織る

レタスのような頭の少女たちは
　　　　　摘んだ
ばかりの草花を並べて

太陽のような笑いを糸にして
夢に縁飾りを付ける

COBBLESTONES

of Vilnius
unfold centuries

every morning
before the city wakes
the lonely walk

near fading lilacs
a woman rustles
through rubbish

she sorts the bins
into plastic bags

sits on the park bench

feeds the birds
                her hunger

ヴィリニュスの

石畳の栗石は
幾世紀も歴史を紐解いている

街の目覚める前の
夜明けごとに
萎れゆくライラックの

そばを通って歩む
孤独な娘が
屑箱をかさこそ鳴らして

瓶をより分け
ポリ袋に入れる

公園のベンチに腰を下ろし

小鳥に餌をやる
　　　　　彼女のひもじさ

ON DRAGON'S SHIP

she swirls
with sun spirals
in her hair
she captures
the cornflower sky

and looks at sleep
through window ruins

龍の船に乗って

彼女の髪の中で
渦巻く太陽とともに
彼女は舞い踊り
蒼穹の
矢車草を捕まえ

廃墟の窓越しに
眠りを見つめる

THE BELL

left its church
absent–mindedly
in search of lost
            hours

鐘は

その教会を去り
虚ろな心のまま
失われた時を
　　　　求める

EVERY MORNING

at the break of dawn
with hand made brooms
men and women
sweep the streets
of the city

at intervals men sit
by building fences
                 to smoke

women's faces
lined in hardship
gather their
loaded dust

毎朝

夜明けになると
手作りの箒を持って
男たちや女たちが
街の通りを
掃いている

時々男たちは建物の
柵の傍に腰を下ろして
　　　　　　煙草を吸う

苦しい生活を刻まれた
女たちの顔には
集められたゴミが
積もっている

THE WIND'S MOAN

fills the sky
with raven wings

blood maple
spreads
across fading sun

birds collage
opens to chorus

風の呻きが

大空を満たし
大鳥が羽を広げる

血の色をした楓の葉が
薄れゆく太陽の顔を
覆ってゆく

鳥のコラージュが
コーラスに合わせて開く

LONG WHITE NIGHT

walks the ceiling

doors echo
all they've heard

windows stare
into an empty street

a Persian cat
ghosts the footpath

Scelsi's *Anahit*

enters the walls

眠れぬ夜が裳裾を引き

天井を歩く

木霊するドアー
誰もが聞き耳を立て

窓たちは
虚ろな街路を見つめる

ペルシャ猫が一匹
歩道を忍び歩く

スケルシの「アナヒット」が

壁を抜けてくる

スケルシ：Giacinto Scelsi（1905－88）
イタリアの作曲家。「アナヒット」は彼の作品名でヴィナスのエジプト名。
リジアはスケルシと呼ぶが、Google ではジャチントウ・シェルシとなっている。

SOMETHING IS SAID

But in this world and this time I must
reach out to you in words.

J. M. COETZEE

何かが語られているが

今のこの世では
私は言葉で語るしかないのだ

J. M. COETZEE

J. M. COETZEE : クッツェー（1940-）
南アフリカの作家。2003年ノーベル文学賞受賞。

IN THAT SPHERE

of transparency
dreams spin
their phantoms

with each stroke of a Hand
something is said

透明なあの天空では

夢が
その幻想を
紡いでいる

手のひと振りごとに
何かが語られる

THAT SUN FILLED MORNING

you left
a sheen on my skin

I still feel
its golden warmth

this evening
I look for you
in the pages
of this book

あの頃　太陽は朝を満たし

　　　　　　　　　　貴方は私の
肌に煌きを残して去っていった

私は今も
あの金色の暖かさを感じている

この夕べ
私はあなたを
この書物のページの中に
求めている

PAPER SOAKS

the remains
of an instant

I trade
my ribcage
for the word

言葉の言い残したものを

ページの空白が
吸収する

私は
肋骨の内側を
言葉と取り引きする

BAREFOOT DUSK

tramples
knotted thoughts

floods the moonstone
of my fingers

夕暮れが裸足で

固く結ばれた思いを
踏みにじり

私の指の
ムーンストーンを押し流す

A SHADE

passed the window
with book in hand

I stirred

the gums watched
you walk
through gates
of transparent bone
into luminous space

as we wove words
under the wisteria
the sun quiver
broke our shadows

影が

本を片手に
窓を横切った

身じろぎする私

透明な骨の
戸口を通り抜け
眩い空間へ歩むあなたを
私の歯茎が
見つめ

藤棚の下で
私たちは言葉を紡ぎ
太陽は震え
私たちの影を破った

YOU STOOD

like an island
among people

your breath
spread into mist

you stood out
from the crowd

words slowly swam
from your shore

貴方は立っていた

群衆の中に浮かぶ
島のように

あなたの吐く息が
靄の中に広がってゆく

あなたは群衆から
抜け出して立っていた

あなたの岸辺から
言葉がゆっくりと泳ぎだした

WALKING THE FIELD

I become the flowers
turn greener than grass

your silence
is a perfume
about me

野原を歩いていると

私は花になり
草よりもっと緑になる

あなたの沈黙は
私を包む
香水です

THE LONGING

that melts into prayer
sparks into hope

憧れは

祈りの中に溶け込み
希望となって煌く

AT NIGHT

stars cling
to my soul

silver footprints
splash
forgotten streams

the full moon
knows a word
can cancel the dark

夜になると

星たちが
私の心に纏わる

銀色の足跡が
忘却の流れに
弾ける

満月は知っている
言葉が
闇を駆逐すると

A THOUGHT OF EARTH

upon a seat of sky

and you are here
and you are here

大地の思いは

雲のシートに

そして貴方はここに
そして貴方はここに

IN THE SUN

Eucalyptus silver arms
embraced our bodies

the scent of the leaves
glowed on our hands

we saw beyond our eyes

陽光の中で

銀色に輝くユーカリの腕が
私たちの体を抱きすくめ

その葉の香りが
手の中で白光を放つのが

視野の彼方に見えた

COPTIC LIGHT

Forgive the voice I beat
like a drum
on the edge
of a snowflake

CHRISTIAN LOIDL

コプトの灯火よ

鈴蘭水仙の
　花びらの縁で
　　太鼓のように
　　　打ち鳴らす私の声を許したまえ

CHRISTIAN LOIDL

CHRISTIAN LOIDL：クリスチャン・ロイドル（1957-2001）
オーストリアの詩人・翻訳家・批評家。リジアは 1992 年 5 月、リトア
ニアの春の詩祭で彼に会い、感銘を受けた。彼は 2001 年 12 月、突然亡
くなった。「コプトの灯火よ」の章は彼に捧げるリジアの追悼の詩である。

THE DESOLATE COURTYARD

with barren peach tree
claimed your body

a broken window
scattered written notes
hold the night's secret

summers will taste of sorrow

perhaps in some remote place
I'll stumble across a shadow
bearing your light

荒れ果てた中庭

不毛の桃の木が
お前の体を求めている

破れた窓
覚書の紙切れが散らばり
夜の秘密を抱える

夏は悲しみの味がする

多分どこか離れた場所で
あなたの光をかざして
私はよろめきながら影を横切るだろう

FACELESS WIND

carves the face
where crevasse's hold
the secret

顔のない風が

顔を刻み
そこではクレバスが秘密を
　　　　　　　抱えている

WORDS OPEN WOUNDS

I drown in a tear

言葉が傷口を開く

私は涙の海に沈む

AS YOU LAY

in the courtyard
stars lit you a shrine
in the dark from snow
white lysantheums

what happened that night
when shattered glass framed
the contours of my disturbed sleep
through a thicket of grey pain
in the courtyard of Vereinsgasse

in that cold winter night
bleak apartment walls
orphaned your body

candles sprung from earth
when dawn saw
your blood stains
on snow

貴方が中庭で

倒れていたとき
星たちは貴方を照らし
白いリサンテウムの
社を闇の中に浮かばせる

あの夜何が起こったのか
あの時ヴェレインス通りの中庭の
灰色の苦痛の茂みを抜けて
割れたガラスが
私の眠りを突然鮮明にした

あの凍える冬の夜
荒れ果てたアパートの壁が
貴方の体を孤児とした

ロウソクが何本も大地から芽を出し
その時曙は見た
貴方の血潮が点々と
雪の上に滴るのを

ヴェレインス通り：クリスチャン・ロイドルが住んでいたところ。

WITH TEARS

I follow the contour
of your face

listen
to the voice
of no return

涙で

私はあなたの顔の
輪郭をなぞり

返るはずもない
声に
耳を傾ける

IN MOURNING DRESS

I walk the Praterstrasse
among glowing candles

Morton Feldman's *Coptic Light*
rustles through trees

suddenly I stop
startled at your image
fastened to a crossroad sign

slowly you come towards me
with lilies black and roses white

the turning Ferris wheel's
lament tells of fate

melting wax trickles
on the snowdrift road
music swells the stillness
snow covers remnants of words

喪服をまとい

私はプラタ通りを歩む
煌めくロウソクの中

モートン・フェルドマンの
「コプトの灯火」が木立の中をそよぐ

突如私は立ち止まる
あなたの姿が十字路の信号灯に
縛りつけられている

ゆっくりとあなたは私の方に下りてくる
黒い百合と白い薔薇を持って

回転する巨大な観覧車は
運命の悲しさを語っている

熔けるロウソクが
雪の吹きだまる道路にゆっくりと滴り
調べが静寂を膨らませ
雪が言葉の名残を覆ってゆく

you say my name
place roses on my head
lilies at my feet

no bird's song saddens the air

あなたは私の名を呼び
バラを私の頭に置き
ユリを足元に置く

辺りの空気を乱す鳥の声もない

モートン・フェルドマン：Morton Feldman（1926－1987）
アメリカの作曲家。「コプトの灯火」は彼の最晩年の作。

COLOUR DIED

under snow

but I search
for your form

touch stone

feel shiver of
leaf and flower

色は死んだ

雪の下で

だけど私は探す
あなたの姿を

石に触れ

葉や花の
震えを感じる

PERHAPS IT'S A DREAM

only a dream, I'll wake, find you are not dead, it's
only a bad dream, a dream of faraway murmurs,
tears blanket the words. I pace the night, I walk
into night, time tosses and turns, in no time, out
of time, grief pierces my bones, I read the words
again, and again, endless fence of thoughts, tears
swell the night, many nights I wince with faraway
wolves, it can't be true, my bones know it's true,
in silence, out of silence, I pillow talk through
tears, wrestle with walls, no walls, only shadows,
white shadows, only night, I cut through air, gaze
into stars, if only I had words, the right words, no
words, only silence, it's only a dream, the mirror
curves, minutes waver, I hear your voice, a voice of
rose and dust, a voice of sun and ice, no voice

多分夢だろう

ほんの夢なんだ　私は目覚めている　あなたは死んでなんかいない　それはちょっとした悪い夢なんだ　遠いところのつぶやきのような夢なんだ　涙が言葉を毛布で包み込む　私は夜を歩む　夜の中へ歩む　時が跳ね　時がトンボを切り　間に合わない　時間切れだ　悲しみが私の骨を貫く　私はあの言葉を読む　何度も何度も繰り返し　果てしなく続く柵のような想い　涙が夜を膨らます　夜毎　私は見えない狼の群れに立ちすくむ　そんなはずはない　私の骨は本当のことを知っている　声に出せず　沈黙の中で　涙の中で私は睦言を交わし壁と格闘し　いや壁などない　影だ　白い影だ　ただの夜だ　私は空気を切り裂き　星の群れに目を凝らす　もし私に言葉があるなら　正しい言葉が　いや言葉なんか無い　沈黙だけだ　これは夢に過ぎない　鏡は歪み　時は揺れている　あなたの声が聞こえる　バラと塵の声　太陽と氷の声　声じゃない

memory weaves into backbone eye, thoughts spike,
weigh down by words, no words, only words, until
they find me, in night rainbows, my pen weeps, it's
only a dream, no dream, all is a dream

with reference to Samuel Beckett's „The Unnamable"

記憶が背骨に目を織り込む　想いが楔を打ち込み
言葉で押しつぶす　言葉じゃない　いや言葉だけ
だ　やがて奴らが私を見つける　夜の虹の中　私
のペンはすすり泣く　夢に過ぎない　いや夢なん
かじゃない　全ては夢

　　サムエル・ベケットの「名づけえぬもの」に関連して

RAIN POURS

no memory
grey cloud
changing cloud

all cloud

雨は土砂降り

記憶は無い
灰色の雲
うつろう雲

全て雲

OCEAN BREATH

salts the rocks

the lighthouse
watches birds in
heaven's strangeness

clouds pause after
centuries of wondering

your final flight
chalked white sails
into night sky

海の吐息が

岩礁を塩漬けにする

灯台は
変調する天空の中で
海鳥たちを見守る

雲たちは何世紀もの
放浪の挙句小休止

あなたの最後の飛行が
夜の空に
白い航跡を描く

WATER BOILS

in samovar
near the book shelf

Gould's Bach
lifts the dust
enters wall cracks

words flow in a fugue
our mouths spoke true

window opens
children play
in the courtyard

we slumbered
like wine in seashells

Brandenburg plays
I drink tea
think about poppies

and remember

水が沸騰する

本棚の近く
サモワールの中で

グールドのバッハが
埃を巻き上げ
壁の罅割れに侵入する

言葉は流れて形を成し
我々の口は真実を語る

窓は開き
子供たちは
中庭で遊ぶ

い眠る私たちは
貝殻の中のワイン

ブランデンブルグが流れ
私はお茶を飲み
ケシの花を想う

そして思い出す

グールド：Glenn Herbert Gould (1932−82)
カナダのピアニスト。

Author's Footnote

I met **Christian Loidl**, Dr.phil. (1957-2001: born in Upper Austria) poet, translator and critic at the Spring Poetry Festival in Lithuania (May 1992). I was impressed the way he used his voice in his poetry performance. He likewise was affected by my intuitive feel for space and silence in my reading. (Christian was a practising Tibetan Buddhist). Our meeting resulted in a lengthy inspirational correspondence and intermittent meetings at various poetry festivals and readings. He translated my early poetry into German "Weisse Schatten / White Shadows (Austria, 2000) with an insightful foreword. (A selection from this collection was used by composer Margery Smith for her composition for voice and chamber orchestra and performed with my reading at the Utzon Recital Hall - Sydney Opera House (Oct. 2015).

Christian's words that we are a part of "the eternal poetry space" has stayed with me, despite our various differences. His unexpected tragic death (Dec.2001) and the loss of a friend / mentor shook me profoundly and resulted in the cycle of poems "Coptic Light" (name of composition by Morton Feldman).

I am extremely grateful that Koichi Yakushigawa who I had the great honour to finally meet in Lithuania (Oct. 2014) has translated and published my two latest books "Something is said" and "Thought and Rock" along with earlier works. I have also translated some of his poems (from English, alas). They have graced the front page of the Lithuanian weekly cultural journal "Literature and Art".

My deepest appreciation,   Lidija Šimkutė

クリスチャン・ロイドルのこと

リジア・シムクーテ

1992年5月、リトアニア春の詩祭で私は初めてクリスチャン・ロイドルに出会った。彼は1957年にオーストリアに生まれた詩人、批評家、翻訳家であり、チベット仏教の実践家でもあった。

彼が詩を朗読するときの声の使い方に私は強い感銘を受けた。一方彼は私の朗読における間の取りかたに非常な感動を覚えたと言う。その出会い以来、私達はたがいにインスピレーションに満ちた文通を続け、またあちこちで開かれる詩祭や朗読会などでの出会いを重ねてきた。

彼は私の初期の作品を纏めてドイツ語に翻訳し『白い影』と題する詩集にして出版し、極めて洞察力に富んだ序文を書いてくれた。この詩集から選ばれたいくつかの作品はマージェリー・スミスによって作曲され、声楽と室内管弦楽団用に編曲されて2015年10月、シドニー・オペラハウスのリサイタル・ホールで上演され、私もその中で詩の朗読をした。

クリスチャンの、私達は『詩と言う永遠の宇宙』の一部である、という言葉は、私の心の中に様々な互いの相違を超えて生き続けている。2001年12月、彼の思いもよらない悲劇的な死、友人であり尊敬する先達を失った悲しみが私の心を震わし、「コプトの灯火」(これはモートン・フェルドマンの曲名なのだが)と題する一連の作品となった。

RAIN SOUND

It's the enigma of ourselves
that continues to fascinate

EDMOND JABÈS

雨の音

それは謎である我々自身
魅惑し続けるもの

EDMOND JABÈS

EDMOND JABÈS：エドモン・ジャベス（1912−91）
エジプト生まれ。フランス国籍のシュールレアリズムの詩人 。

FLOATING

in rain sound
thoughts are read
before time

eyes come to a head

浮漂しつつ

雨音の中で
想いは纏まらぬまま
読まれている

目が頭の中にやって来る

TO FIND THE MOON

in a fingernail
is easier than to hunt
for the sun in sleep

yet there are days when
the sun is within reach
and the moon keeps
sleepers awake

a sky beneath the lidded eyes

lets moon and sun disappear

this is where dreams
are gathered out of sight

月を見つけることは

指の爪なら易しいが
眠りの中で太陽
を追い求めるのは難しい

けれども太陽が手の届くところに在り
月が眠ろうとする人を
目覚まし続けるそんな時が
あるものだ

瞼で覆われた目の下で

空は月も陽も隠す

其処は夢が視野の外で
凝り固まるところ

CREEPING WIND

from the cloister
opens heavy
oak doors

where tarot cards
and crystal balls
are read

風が回廊から

忍び込んで
重たい樫の
扉を開く

そこはタロットのカードと
水晶の球が
読まれるところ

THE BALTIC STORM

blew away chimneys
and roof antennas

trees shook
as evening sun swept
sidewalks of passersby

leaves shed tears
on tree iron rosettes
              in the streets

a sparrow dropped
a wing in my mailbox

バルチックの嵐が

屋根のアンテナや
煙突を吹き飛ばし

夕日が
歩み去る人々の歩道を
掃き渡る頃　並木は震え

木の葉が街路樹の
ロゼットに
　　　　　　涙を散らす

雀が羽を一枚
私の郵便受けに落としてゆく

MOODS OF THE SEA

flow into pen

sketch
the dream
on waters of sleep

移り気な海が

ペンに流れ込み

眠りの波間に
夢を
スケッチする

for Marija Gimbutas

IN RAINY SUMMER

walking the banks of Vilna
I came across your smile
in the trunk of a tree

the sky opened

a snow–drift voice rustled
from the mountain ash

time stood still
you were here

let the startled whispers
echo to Topanga Canyon
and the trodden desert path
where our palms flamed
in chtonic moon light

マリヤ　ギンブタスに捧ぐ

雨の夏

ビルナの堤を歩いていると
並木の幹の中に
あなたの微笑みを見つけた

空は広々と広がっている

山の巨木から落ちる
雪の塊が葉擦れの音を立てる

ときは静かに立ち竦み
あなたはここにいる

思わず漏らす仰天声を
トパンガ渓谷に木霊させ
掌が不気味な月の光に
縁どられる
荒地の小道に響かせよ

Marija Gimbutas : マリヤ・ギンブタス (1921−94)
リトアニアの考古学者。

ROUND THE SPHERE

of daydreams
my curtain self

私のカーテンよ

白昼夢の天空を
張り巡らせよ

WIND KNOCKS

on doors

street traffic
hums
a monotonous beat

rain
drops
fill
the beggar's
bowl

風がノックする

並んだドア

街路をゆく車の
鼻歌が
単調なリズムを流す

雨の
小粒が
乞食の
椀を
満たす

ENIGMATIC

letters
of the mind
write themselves
on pillow

謎めいた

心の
文字が
枕に
浮かぶ

A LASTING SONG

He that sings a lasting song
thinks in a marrow bone

W. B. YEATS

終わりなき歌

終わりなき歌を歌う人は
骨髄の中で思う

W. B. YEATS

W. B. YEATS：イエイツ（1865－1939）
アイルランドの詩人。

THE EAGLE RISES

skeleton columns
shimmer
in fern flower* wind

thought is etched
into bone

* according to Lithuanian legend the fern flower blooms
briefly at midnight on the summer solstice-St. John's eve
when remnants of ancient pagan rites are celebrated.

鷲が立ち上がる

骸骨の柱が
羊歯の花*にそよぐ風の中で
微かに光る

思いが骨に
刻印される

*リトアニアの伝説によれば、羊歯の花は夏至、聖ヨハネ前夜祭の
真夜中に短時間咲くと言われている。またそれは異教の祭典が開
かれる時（魔女が活躍する時）でもある。

THE MILKY WAY

lights the village
under night sky

chimney smoke
softens the gravel path

fish scale-sheen spreads
across sea grass

the windows
don't know they
are being looked at

天の川が

夜空の下の
村を照らす

煙突の煙が
砂利道を宥_{なだ}める

煌く魚の鱗が
海藻の間に広がる

窓は
見られているのが
自分だとは知らない

CLOUDS FALL

into the sea
and emerge as islands

white sails
drown in fog

birds shriek
horizons vanish

雲は海に

落ちるが
島となって現れる

白い帆が
霧の中に消える

海鳥が鳴き
水平線が消える

CAR DIN

carries tedium

cement blocks
fence the heat

scattered palms
fan air against
white hot blindness

shadows scurry
in dust

your turn
carries
my face away

車の喧騒が

退屈を運んでくる

セメントのブロックが
熱気を遮断する

散らばった棕櫚の葉が
熱気に白く眩んだ眼に
涼風を送る

影が慌てて
埃の中を駆ける

君が振り返ると
私の顔が
そっぽを向く

IN THE STREETS

of Budapest
I hear your voice
from the tram's
iron beat

the sun
pierces my mind
like a church
with steeples

ブダペストの

街中で
君の声が聞こえる
市街電車の
鉄輪のきしみの中

太陽は
心の中まで差し込む
まるで教会の
尖塔だ

THE WAITRESS'S SMILE

flavours plain rice

with five-petalled touch
she pours green tea
into lotus cups

ウェイトレスの微笑みが

只のご飯に風味を添える

花弁のような指を添え
蓮のコップに
緑の茶を注ぐ

FADED PALM

creaks near a dingy KGB bar
in New York city

vodka is poured
into unwashed glasses
by caviar headed women
in tight scaly dresses

men with glassy eyes
shirtless
tattooed
argue their life away

silence hangs
like fish-net stockings

色褪せた棕櫚の葉が

ニューヨークの薄汚れた
KGB バーの傍で悲鳴を上げる

薄汚れたままのグラスに
ウォッカが注がれ
傍には鱗のようにピッチリとした
ドレスの女たちがキャビアのような頭をしている

生気のない眼の男たちは
もろ肌脱ぎで
刺青を見せ
人生をがなり立てている

ぶら下がる沈黙は
投網のようなストッキング

KGB は旧ソ連の秘密警察、リトアニアは一時期ソ連の支配下に在った。
棕櫚の葉は勝利の栄冠。

ON MARKET DAYS

fish sleep on ice

how many turns
does it take
to bury the dead
in light year deep

there is no time like forever

市の立つ日に

魚は氷の上で眠る

この死魚たちを
埋葬するには
たっぷり何光年
かかるのだろう

永遠という時間はない

WHERE CITIES END

— nests fly

ominous bird song
emerges as grass sings

music outlives
people
and trees

都会の終わる処

―― 巣は飛び立つ

不吉な鳥の歌が
草が歌うように湧く

音楽は生き延びる
人類よりも
樹木よりも

ERASE WORDS

from memory

elsewhere — is here
what is not — is born again

re-enters every cell
and sap from
the stamen of sound

言葉を消せ

記憶から

何処かで ── 此処か
否の存在が ── 再生する

全ての細胞に戻り直し
音の精髄から
精気を吸い取れ

Lidija Šimkutė was born in a small village in Samogitia, Lithuania in 1942. After WWII she spent her early childhood as a refugee in displaced persons camps in Germany; she arrived in Australia in 1949. She extended her studies by correspondence in Lithuanian language, literature and folklore (1973-1978) through the Lithuanian Language Institute in Chicago, USA and went to Vilnius University, Lithuania in 1977 and 1987.

She worked professionally as a dietitian. Since her retirement in 2001 she divides her time between the two countries. She has travelled widely.

L. Šimkutė's poetry publications **in Lithuanian**: *The Second Longing*, 1978; *Anchors of Memory*, 1982 (USA); *Wind and Roots*, 1991 (Lithuania); **in English**: *The Sun Paints a Sash*, 2000 (USA); **Bilingual**: *Tylos erdvės / Spaces of Silence*, 1999; *Vejo žvilgesys / Wind Sheen*, 2003; *Mintis ir uola / Thought and Rock*, 2008 (Lithuania); *Weiße Schatten / White Shadows*, 2000 (Austria), – translated by Christian Loidl; *Iš toli ir arti / Z bliska i z daleka*,

リジア・シムクーテは 1942 年、リトアニアのサモギチ
アに在る小さな村に生まれた。第二次大戦後、彼女は難
民としてドイツの難民キャンプでその幼少期を過ごした。
1949 年、彼女はオーストラリアに辿りついた。さらに彼
女は通信教育でアメリカのシカゴのリトアニア語学校で
(1973-1978)、リトアニアの言語、文学、民間伝承などを
学び、1977 年と 1987 年にはリトアニアのヴィルニス大学
に学ぶ。

　彼女は栄養学の専門家として働いていた。2001 年に退
職後、彼女は生活を二つの国に分けている。彼女の旅行は
多岐にわたる。

　シムクーテの詩集は、1978 年『第二希望』／ 1982 年『記
憶の錨』(USA)、1991 年『風と根っ子』(リトアニア) が
リトアニア語；2000 年『太陽がサッシを彩る』(USA) は
英語、1999 年『沈黙の空間』／ 2003 年『きらめく風』／
2008 年『想いと磐』(リトアニア)、2000 年『白い影』(オー
ストリア) は、英語とリトアニア語の 2 ヵ国語で書かれて
いる。

2003, (Poland) translated by Sigitas Birgelis.

Šimkutė writes in Lithuanian and English and is published in various literary journals and anthologies in Australia, Lithuania and elsewhere including *The World Poetry Almanac*, Mongolia (2008, 2010), and *The Turnrow Anthology of Contemporary Australian Poetry*, 2013 (USA). Her poetry has been translated into fifteen languages and she has translated Australian poetry/ prose and other works into Lithuanian.

Šimkutė has read her poetry in various countries and at International Poetry Festivals.

Lithuanian and Australian composers and artists have used her poetry in their compositions for ensembles and their works in Lithuania, Australia and other European countries.

In 2002 her poetry was read and choreographed for modern dance perfomances in Australia, Lithuania and other European countries. In 2005 her poetry collection *Spaces of Silence* was choreographed for stage with author reading, Japanese flute, percussion and modern dance for various theatres in Lithuania.

Her poem *My Father* was short-listed for *Poem of the Millennium at the Australian Poetry Festival in* 2004, and she was one of the laureates in a *Haiku competition* at the *Druskininkai Poetic Fall in Lithuania* (2009).

Lidija Šimkutė has received a number of literary grants from Australia Council Literature Board, South Australia Department for the Arts and the Australian Lithuanian Foundation.

シムクーテはリトアニア語と英語とで著作し、オースト
ラリア、リトアニア、その他モンゴル人民共和国の『世界
詩集年鑑』(2008, 2010)、『オーストラリア現代詩選』(2013)
といった様々な文芸誌やアンソロジーに発表している。彼
女の詩は 15 ヵ国語に翻訳され、また彼女はオーストラリ
アの詩や散文をリトアニア語に翻訳している。

シムクーテはまた、様々な国や様々な国際詩祭などで自
作の朗読をしている。リトアニアやオーストラリアの作曲
家や音楽家たちは様々な国でのアンサンブルの構成の中に
彼女の作品を組み込んでいる。

2002 年には、彼女の詩がオーストラリアやリトアニア、
およびヨーロッパの諸国で朗読され、現代ダンスの振り付
けがされている。2005 年には、彼女の詩集『沈黙の空間』
が作者の朗読、日本の尺八、パーカッションと共にモダー
ンダンスが振り付けられて、舞台に上演された。

彼女の詩「私の父」は『2004 年オーストラリアミレニ
アム詩祭の詩』の予選を通過した。また彼女は『ドラスキ
ニンカイ秋の詩祭 2009』における俳句コンペで表彰者の
一人となった。

リジア・シムクーテは南オーストラリア州文芸委員会や
オーストラリア・リトアニア財団などから様々な助成金を
受けている。

訳者あとがき

　またしてもリジア・シムクーテ（どうやらリトアニアで体験したところに依れば、Ｓの上にアクセントの記がある文字は、英語のＳよりSHに近い発音のようだ。シュムクーテの方が近いかもしれない）さんの詩集を翻訳出版することにした。これも、以前、関西詩人協会のホームページに掲載したものだが、やはり何度読み返しても怪しい処は直らないし、判らぬところは判らぬままになっている。だが格好をつけるために、前後を考えてなんとか丸く収めているところがある。拙い翻訳をご寛恕いただき、ご教示いただければありがたいと思う。

　前の詩集に引き続き、彼女の詩はやはり私には判りやすい。すんなりと心に入ってくるようだ。説明せよと言われると困るのだが、なんとなくわかる気がする。42 – 43頁の作品が、この詩集を読み解くカギとなるだろう。言葉をいくら並べても、言いつくせないものが残る。それがページの空白の部分に漂っているのだろう。西洋の絵画は画面を全て色と形で覆い尽くすが、日本の絵画には空白の部分がたくさん残されている。空白は何も無いただの空白ではなく、そこにこそ色と形では表わし得ないものが表現されているのではないだろうか。色即是空、空即是色と悟り済ましてみてもいいかもしれない。それはひょっとすると、52 – 53頁にある「憧れ」のように「希望」と言う名の「祈

り」となるかもしれない。「祈り」に頼る儚さ、と言ってしまえば身も蓋もない。だが私たちは、何時もそういった儚さに目をつむって、頼っていはしないか。例えば「平和」という言葉がそれではないだろうか。それより、いったいこの世に確かなもの、なんて存在するのだろうか。

58 - 59頁を見給え。この不確かさこそ真の存在ではないだろうか。私たちは誰もが文字を書き続けているが、果たして文字が何を表してくれるというのか。キーボードから叩き出される文字のほかに謎めいた文字があることを誰もが心得ているはずだ。またしても私には、あの聖書に在る「文字は殺しますが」という言葉が頭の中をガンガン駆け巡る。

リジアさんの詩は、謎解きの面白さだけではなく、常に挑発的だ。

2016年1月22日
薬師川虹一記

訳者略歴

薬師川虹一（やくしがわ・こういち）

1929 年生まれ。1954 年同志社大学大学院（英文学専攻）文学修士。
現在、同志社大学名誉教授。
「日本詩人クラブ」「関西詩人協会」「京都写真芸術家協会」「NPO
日本写道協会」会員／詩誌「RAVINE」編集・発行同人

〈受賞歴〉
1997 年 7 月　京都市芸術文化協会賞
2010 年 4 月　瑞宝中綬章
2014 年 10 月　日本翻訳家協会より翻訳特別賞

〈著書〉『イギリス・ロマン派の研究』、『ヒーニーの世界』
〈訳書〉『障害児の治療と教育』
〈共訳〉『フィリップ・ラーキン詩集』、『シェイマス・ヒーニー全詩
　　　　集 1966 ～ 1995 年』、ヒーニー『水準器』、『電燈』、『郊外線
　　　　と環状線』、『さ迷えるスウィニー』、『人間の鎖』
〈詩集〉『疲れた犬のいる風景』
　　　　『詩と写真―石佛と語る』他
〈訳詩集〉リジア・シムクーテ『想いと磐／ THOUGHT AND ROCK』

CONTENTS

OUTLIVING PEOPLE AND TREES
TOMAS VENCLOVA   4

CORNFLOWER SKY   14

A BIRD CALL...   16

HOW BEAUTIFUL...   18

TIME LINGERS...   20

SCARVED WOMEN...   22

COBBLESTONES...   24

ON DRAGON'S SHIP...   26

THE BELL...   28

EVERY MORNING...   30

THE WIND'S MOAN...   32

LONG WHITE NIGHT...   34

SOMETHING IS SAID   36

IN THAT SPHERE...   38

THAT SUN FILLED MORNING...   40

PAPER SOAKS...   42

BAREFOOT DUSK...   44

目 次

人を超え樹を超えて生きる
トマス・ヴェンクロヴァ　5

矢車草の空　15

鳥の叫びが...　17

なんと美しいのだろう...　19

時はそぞろに...　21

スカーフを巻いた女たちが...　23

ヴィリニュスの...　25

龍の船に乗って...　27

鐘は...　29

毎朝...　31

風の呻きが...　33

眠れぬ夜が裳裾を引き...　35

何かが語られているが　37

透明なあの天空では...　39

あの頃　太陽は朝を満たし...　41

言葉の言い残したものを...　43

夕暮れが裸足で...　45

A SHADE... 46

YOU STOOD... 48

WALKING THE FIELD... 50

THE LONGING... 52

AT NIGHT... 54

A THOUGHT OF EARTH... 56

IN THE SUN... 58

COPTIC LIGHT 60

THE DESOLATE COURTYARD... 62

FACELESS WIND... 64

WORDS OPEN WOUNDS... 66

AS YOU LAY... 68

WITH TEARS... 70

IN MOURNING DRESS... 72

COLOUR DIED... 76

PERHAPS IT'S A DREAM... 78

RAIN POURS... 82

OCEAN BREATH... 84

WATER BOILS... 86

Author's Footnote 88

影が ... 47

貴方は立っていた ... 49

野原を歩いていると ... 51

憧れは ... 53

夜になると ... 55

大地の思いは ... 57

陽光の中で ... 59

コプトの灯火よ　　61

荒れ果てた中庭 ... 63

顔のない風が ... 65

言葉が傷口を開く ... 67

貴方が中庭で ... 69

涙で ... 71

喪服をまとい ... 73

色は死んだ ... 77

多分夢だろう ... 79

雨は土砂降り ... 83

海の吐息が ... 85

水が沸騰する ... 87

クリスチャン・ロイドルのこと　89

RAIN SOUND 90

FLOATING... 92

TO FIND THE MOON... 94

CREEPING WIND... 96

THE BALTIC STORM... 98

MOODS OF THE SEA... 100

IN RAINY SUMMER... 102

ROUND THE SPHERE... 104

WIND KNOCKS... 106

ENIGMATIC... 108

A LASTING SONG 110

THE EAGLE RISES... 112

THE MILKY WAY... 114

CLOUDS FALL... 116

CAR DIN... 118

IN THE STREETS... 120

THE WAITRESS'S SMILE... 122

FADED PALM... 124

ON MARKET DAYS... 126

WHERE CITIES END... 128

ERASE WORDS... 130

About the Author 134

雨の音　91

浮漂しつつ ...　93

月を見つけることは ...　95

風が回廊から ...　97

バルチックの嵐が ...　99

移り気な海が ...　101

雨の夏 ...　103

私のカーテンよ ...　105

風がノックする ...　107

謎めいた ...　109

終わりなき歌　111

鷲が立ち上がる ...　113

天の川が ...　115

雲は海に ...　117

車の喧騒が ...　119

ブダペストの ...　121

ウェイトレスの微笑みが ...　123

色褪せた棕櫚の葉が ...　125

市の立つ日に ...　127

都会の終わる処 ...　129

言葉を消せ ...　131

訳者あとがき　138

訳者略歴　141